THE JEMIMA PUDDLE-DUCK™ TREASURY

Fun to Read and Do

with

Stories and Puzzles

From the authorized animated series based on
the original tales by
BEATRIX POTTER™

Bloomsbury Books
in association with Frederick Warne

BLOOMSBURY BOOKS
IN ASSOCIATION WITH FREDERICK WARNE

Published by the Penguin Group
Penguin Books Ltd, 27 Wrights Lane, London W8 5TZ, England
Penguin Books USA Inc., 375 Hudson Street, New York, N.Y. 10014, USA
Penguin Books Australia Ltd, Ringwood, Victoria, Australia
Penguin Books Canada Ltd, 10 Alcorn Avenue, Toronto, Ontario, Canada M4V 3B2
Penguin Books (N.Z.) Ltd, 182-190 Wairau Road, Auckland 10, New Zealand

Penguin Books Ltd, Registered Offices: Harmondsworth, Middlesex, England

Bloomsbury Books, an imprint of the Godfrey Cave Group, 42 Bloomsbury Street, London WC1B 3QJ

This edition first published 1994
1 3 5 7 9 10 8 6 4 2

Universal Copyright Notice:
Illustrations from *The World of Peter Rabbit and Friends* TM animated television series made by Grand
Slamm Partnership, Jumping Jack Animation Ltd, & Stuart Brooks Animation Ltd, and produced by T.V.
Cartoons Ltd for Frederick Warne & Co.
Copyright © Frederick Warne & Co., 1992,1993
This edition copyright © Frederick Warne & Co. 1994

ISBN 1 85471 2594

Printed and bound in Great Britain by William Clowes Limited, Beccles and London

CONTENTS

WELCOME TO
THE JEMIMA PUDDLE-DUCK™ TREASURY

On this page, meet your new friends.

This is Jemima Puddle-duck, who decides to make a nest far away from the farm. She's really a rather foolish duck. You can find out about her narrow escape on page 12.

This sandy-whiskered gentleman is most polite and charming, but if he asks you to a dinner-party - don't go!

If you ask dear Mrs Tiggy-winkle very nicely, she might wash and iron your pocket handkins for you. Look for a little door in the hillside, knock once, twice - and she may invite you in for a cup of tea!

This is Lucie, who lives at a farm called Little-town. She's a good little girl - only she will keep losing her pocket handkins! You can read about her visit to Mrs Tiggy-winkle's home on page 28.

The tailor of Gloucester sits in his little shop, cross-legged on a table, and sews all day long while the light lasts. Read his story on page 44 to find out how he grew quite rich, and became well-known for the neat stitches of his button-holes.

Simpkin lives with the tailor of Gloucester, and keeps house for him. Simpkin is very fond of mice - although he gives them no satin for coats!

What a funny sight it is to see a brood of ducklings with a hen! The farmer's wife would not let Jemima Puddle-duck hatch her own eggs.

'I wish to hatch my own eggs; I will hatch them all by myself,' quacked Jemima Puddle-duck. So she decided to make a nest right away from the farm.

JEMIMA PUDDLE-DUCK'S STORY

Jemima Puddle-duck was annoyed, because the farmer's wife would not let her hatch her own eggs.

She tried to hide her eggs, but they were always found and

carried off. Jemima Puddle-duck became quite desperate. She determined to make a nest right away from the farm. She set off on a fine spring afternoon, wearing a shawl and a poke bonnet.

Jemima Puddle-duck flew beautifully when she had got a good start. She skimmed along over the tree-tops until she saw a clearing in the middle of a wood.

Jemima alighted rather heavily, and began to waddle about in search of a convenient dry nesting-place. She rather fancied a tree-stump amongst some tall fox-gloves.

But - seated upon the stump, she was startled to find an elegantly dressed gentleman reading a newspaper

The gentleman looked curiously at Jemima - 'Madam, have you lost your way?' said he. Jemima thought him mighty civil and handsome. She explained that she was trying to find a convenient dry nesting-place.

'My dear Madam, I have a sackful of feathers in my wood-shed. You may sit there as long as you like,' said the bushy long-tailed gentleman.

There was a tumble-down shed at the back of the house. The gentleman opened the door, and showed Jemima in. Jemima Puddle-duck was rather surprised to find that the shed was full of feathers. But it was very comfortable; and she made a nest without any trouble at all.

Jemima Puddle-duck came every afternoon; she laid nine eggs in the nest. The foxy gentleman admired them immensely.

At last Jemima told him that she intended to begin to sit on her eggs until they hatched. 'Madam, before you commence your tedious sitting, let us have a dinner-party all to ourselves! May I ask you to bring up some herbs and

onions from the farm-garden to make, er . . . a savoury omelette?' said the hospitable gentleman with sandy whiskers.

Jemima Puddle-duck was a simpleton; she quite unsuspectingly went round nibbling off snippets of all the different sorts of herbs that are used for stuffing roast duck.

'What are you doing with those onions?' asked Kep, the collie dog. 'Where do you go every afternoon by yourself, Jemima Puddle-duck?'

Jemima told him the whole story.

Jemima Puddle-duck
set off for the last time.
She flew over the
wood, and alighted
opposite the house of
the bushy long-tailed gentleman.

He was waiting for her. He sniffed the
air, and kept glancing uneasily around
him. 'Come into the house as soon as you
have looked at your eggs. Give me the
herbs. Be sharp!'

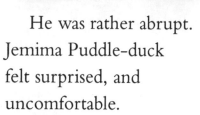

He was rather abrupt.
Jemima Puddle-duck
felt surprised, and
uncomfortable.

While she was inside
someone with a black
nose sniffed at the
bottom of the shed door,
and then locked it.

Jemima became much
alarmed.

Then there was the most awful noise - barking, baying, growls and howls, squealing, and groans. And nothing more was ever seen of that foxy gentlemen. Presently Kep opened the door of the shed, and let out Jemima Puddle-duck. Unfortunately the puppies rushed in and gobbled up all the eggs before he could stop them.

Jemima Puddle-duck was escorted home in tears on account of those eggs.

She laid some more in June, and she was permitted to keep them herself: but only four of them hatched.

Jemima Puddle-duck said that it was because of her nerves; but she had always been a bad sitter.

When Jemima Puddle-duck came out, the sandy-whiskered gentleman was sitting on a log reading the newspaper - at least he had it spread out, but he was looking over the top of it. He said he loved eggs and ducklings; he should be proud to see a fine nestful in his wood-shed.

JEMIMA PUDDLE-DUCK

Paint or colour this picture of Jemima Puddle-duck talking to the sandy-whiskered gentleman.

1 A DINNER PARTY

Jemima Puddle-duck has told the sandy-whiskered
gentleman that she is ready to sit on her eggs until they
hatch. Poor Jemima! He has invited her to a dinner-party,
but she doesn't realise that she is to be the main course!
This word puzzle contains nine ingredients for the meal.
See if you can find them all.

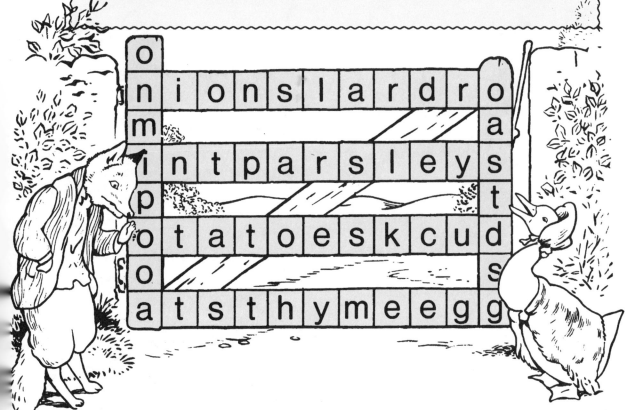

Now fill in the first letter of each of the things drawn here to find
the name of something Jemima is wearing in the puzzle above.

b o n n e t

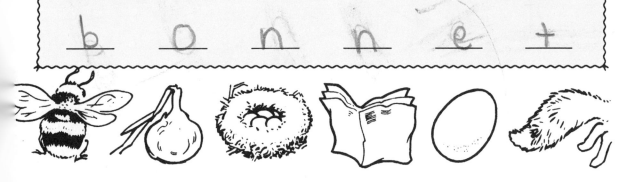

2 A FISHING EXPEDITION

Mr Jeremy Fisher has gone fishing with his friends, Sir Isaac Newton and Mr Alderman Ptolemy Tortoise. Unfortunately, they have got their fishing lines rather tangled! Which of them has caught the fish, who has the shoe and who has the basket?

Help Mr Jeremy Fisher find a path to his lily-leaf boat. You must touch every lily leaf on the way, but only once (mark the way with a pencil so that you don't land on the same leaf twice).

When Jemima described the polite gentleman with sandy whiskers, Kep the collie-dog asked several questions about the wood, and about the exact position of the house and shed. Then he went out, to look for the two fox-hound puppies.

3A PICTURE LETTER

Ginger the cat and Pickles the dog keep a small village shop. They always have a lot of customers, but unfortunately, nobody pays them on time! Here is a letter they have written to Mr Samuel Whiskers about his bill. Can you work it out? (If you want to read about Ginger, Pickles or Mr Samuel Whiskers, you will find a list of the Beatrix Potter Tales at the back of this book.)

My Dear Sir

We have to send you another about the amount of that you

owe us for various goods bought from our We have not been paid

for the bought last week, nor the which has been owing for

 And last week you ordered a of from us as well.

We have also been told by Mrs.  that she saw you taking some

 from the  and putting it in your  . We do not

wish to alarm you, but if you do not send us some soon, we shall have to

call a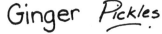

We remain your humble servants,

Ginger Pickles

Ginger and Pickles

26

PAINT A PICTURE

JEMIMA'S NESTING PLACE

Paint or colour this picture of the foxy gentleman ushering Jemima
Puddle-duck into his wood-shed.

MRS TIGGY-WINKLE'S STORY

Once upon a time there was a little girl called Lucie, who lived at a farm called Little-town. She was a good little girl - only she was always losing her pocket-handkerchiefs!

One day little Lucie came into the farm-yard crying - oh, she did

cry so! 'That's three handkins and a pinafore. Oh dear! Definitely gone. Have you seen them, Tabby Kitten?'

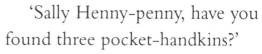

'Sally Henny-penny, have you found three pocket-handkins?'

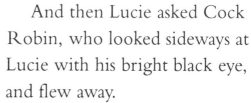

And then Lucie asked Cock Robin, who looked sideways at Lucie with his bright black eye, and flew away.

'Excuse me, sir,' Lucie asked Mr Jeremy Fisher, 'have you seen my pocket handkins or even a pinafore?'

'I'm afraid not, young lady,' he replied.

Presently Lucie came to a spring, bubbling out from the hill-side.

'Goodness! Who could have put such a tiny bucket there - it's no bigger than an egg-cup! And look at those tiny little foot-marks,' remarked Lucie.

But there was something else - a little door in the hillside.

Lucie, knocked - once - twice, and a little frightened voice called out, 'Who's that?'

'I'm Lucie. I didn't mean to startle you, but who are you?' said Lucie. 'And have you seen my pocket-handkins?'

'Oh, yes, if you please'm; my name is Mrs Tiggy-winkle; do make yourself comfortable,' said the little person, as she continued her ironing.

'What's that?' said Lucie – 'that's not my pocket-handkin.'

'Oh no, if you please'm; that's a little scarlet waist-coat belonging to Cock Robin!'

And she ironed it and folded it, and put it on one side.

'There's one of my pocket-handkins!' cried Lucie, searching through the clothes-basket – 'and there's my pinny!'

'Fancy that,' said Mrs Tiggy-winkle, 'they were there all the time. I'll just put the iron over them.'

'There!' exclaimed Mrs Tiggy-winkle proudly, holding up Lucie's newly ironed pinny.

'Oh, that *is* lovely!' said Lucie gratefully.

'Goodness, what are they?' asked Lucie, pointing to some long yellow things.

'Oh, that's a pair of stockings belonging to Sally Henny-penny,' said Mrs Tiggy-winkle.

'There's another handkersniff - but it's red,' said Lucie.

'That one belongs to old Mrs Rabbit; and it did so smell of onions, I've had to wash it separately.'

'Now then, I always have to starch these little dicky shirt-fronts. They're Tom Titmouse's and he's most terrible particular. I'll just hang these up to air. I'd take it very kindly'm if you would hand the things up to me.'

With all the washing hung up to dry, Mrs Tiggy-winkle and Lucie sat down to take some tea.

Then they tied up the clothes in bundles and set off to deliver the clean washing.

The first animals they met were Peter Rabbit and Benjamin Bunny. 'Tell your Mama I've done my very best with the jacket,' said Mrs Tiggy-winkle. Then they delivered a bundle of washing to Mr Jeremy Fisher.

All the little animals and birds were so very much obliged to dear Mrs Tiggy-winkle, and when they came to the bottom of the hill, there was nothing left to carry except Lucie's one little bundle.

Mrs Tiggy-winkle hurried home, not even stopping to give Lucie a bill for the washing. Lucie watched her as she went and wondered, 'But where is your cap and your shawl and your gown? If I didn't know better, Mrs Tiggy-winkle, I would think that you were nothing but a hedgehog!'

'I walked along here the other day with Miss Potter,' said Lucie. 'Perhaps if I go the same way . . . they must be along here somewhere.'

4 WASHING DAY

It's washing day, and all the little animals and birds are very much obliged to dear Mrs Tiggy-winkle for doing their laundry - but, Mrs Tiggy-winkle has pegged everything out on the line, and it has all got into a muddle! In the picture you can see Benjamin Bunny, Pigling Bland, Tom Kitten, Timmy Tiptoes, Jemima Puddle-duck and Samuel Whiskers, all waiting for their clothes. Can you help her work out which clothes belong to each character, and put the right letter in the box beside them?

MRS TIGGY-WINKLE

Paint or colour this picture of Mrs Tiggy-winkle holding a pair of
clean mittens belonging to Tabby Kitten.

'Goodness, look at those tiny little footmarks,' remarked Lucie. And she followed the footprints until she reached a little door in the hillside.

5 PETER RABBIT

Do you remember the story of Peter Rabbit, who nearly came to grief in Mr McGregor's garden? This is a picture of Peter eating radishes, before Mr McGregor has noticed him! There is one difference in detail in each of the six little boxes. Can you spot them? When you have finished, why not colour in the picture? (If you'd like to read more about Peter Rabbit or other Beatrix Potter characters, there is a list of Tales at the back of this book.)

'Now there's a story,' said Mrs Tiggy-winkle, when Lucie held up a tattered blue jacket. 'Young master Peter Rabbit had a narrow escape from Mr McGregor's garden, but his jacket was left behind, and what with the rain and all. . .'

THE TAILOR OF GLOUCESTER

Once upon a time, in the time of swords and periwigs - when gentlemen wore ruffles and gold-laced waistcoats - there was an old tailor who lived in Gloucester.

He sat in his little shop, cross-legged on a table, from morning till dark. All day long while the light lasted he sewed and snippeted.

One bitter cold day near Christmas-time the tailor began to make a coat - a coat of cherry-coloured corded silk. 'The finest of wedding coats for the Mayor of Gloucester who is to be married on Christmas Day in the morning,' he muttered.

The table was littered with snippets of the rich cherry-coloured silk and exquisite taffeta.

'I'm sure I cannot afford to waste the smallest piece,' said the tailor as he continued cutting. 'Too narrow breadths for nought - except waistcoats for mice!'

Unnoticed, little mice retrieved the scraps from his work bench and carried them off.

'I cannot remember when we had silk of such quality on these premises!' exclaimed the little mouse.

The light was fading and the tailor had done his day's work; all the silk and satin lay cut out upon the table. 'All is ready to sew in the morning, except for one item – just one single skein of cherry-coloured twisted silk.'

The tailor locked up his shop and shuffled home through the snow. The mice were more fortunate and did not have to brave the cold. With their secret passages they could run all over town, from house to house, without ever going out into the streets.

The tailor lived alone with his cat, Simpkin, who kept house while the tailor worked. Simpkin was very fond of mice, but he gave them no satin for coats!

'Ah, Simpkin!' exclaimed the tailor as he arrived home. 'I am worn to a ravelling. Take this groat (which is our last fourpence) and buy a penn'orth of bread, a penn'orth of milk and  a penn'orth of sausages.'

'And oh, Simpkin,' remembered the tailor, 'with the last penny buy me a penn'orth of cherry-coloured silk. But do not lose the last penny, Simpkin, for I have no more twist.'

Weary from his day's work, the tailor sat by the fire and began to dream about that beautiful coat.

Suddenly his thoughts were interrupted by little noises coming from the dresser - Tip tap, tip tap tip!

The tailor lifted up a teacup. Out stepped a lady mouse, who gave a deep curtsey. Then, from under the teacups, bowls and basins, stepped more and more little mice!

'This is very peculiar,' remarked the tailor. 'I'll wager this is all Simpkin's doing, the rascal.'

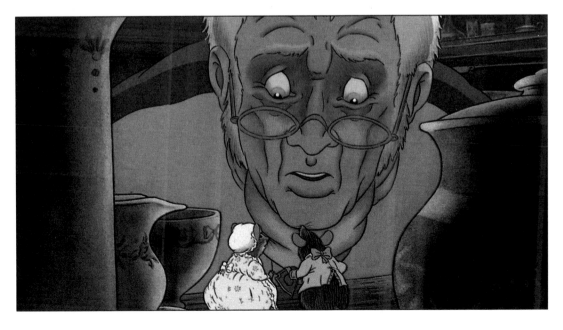

Simpkin returned and opened
the door with an angry 'G-r-r-
miaw!' for he hated the snow. He
looked suspiciously at the dresser
– the cups and jugs had been
moved!

'Simpkin,' asked the tailor
anxiously, 'where is my twist?'
'Where is my mouse?' wondered Simpkin and
quickly hid the twist in the teapot.

'Alack, I am undone,' lamented the tailor and
went sadly to bed.

The poor old tailor was ill with fever. Tossing
and turning in his bed he mumbled, 'No more twist . . . one-and-
twenty button-holes . . . to be finished by noon on Saturday . . . and it
is already Tuesday!'

Indeed, what should become
of the cherry-coloured coat? In
the tailor's shop the embroidered
silk and satin lay ready and cut
out on the table, but who should
come to sew them when the
window was barred and the door
locked?

The tailor lay ill for three days and three nights and then it was Christmas Eve. The moon climbed up over the roofs and chimneys. All the city of Gloucester was fast asleep under the snow.

The cathedral clock struck twelve and Simpkin went out into the night.

Simpkin wandered through the streets but when he turned a corner he saw a glow of light coming from his master's shop. He crept up to the window to peep in.

Inside the shop was a snippeting of scissors and a snappeting of thread and the sound of little mouse voices.

Simpkin miaowed to get in but the door was locked and the key under the tailor's pillow.

He came away from the shop and made his way home. There he found the tailor, without fever and sleeping peacefully. Simpkin felt very ashamed after seeing those good little mice. He took the silk from the teapot and placed it on his master's bed.

'Alack, I am worn to a ravelling, but I have my twist,' said the Tailor of Gloucester. The next morning the tailor went out into the street and made his way to his shop. 'I have my twist,' he said, 'but no more strength or time for this is Christmas Day in the morning.' He opened the door and looked in amazement.

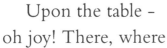

Upon the table -
oh joy! There, where
he had left plain cuttings of silk lay the most
beautiful coat and satin waistcoat.

Everything was finished except one single cherry-coloured
buttonhole, where there was pinned a scrap of paper with these teeny
weeny words - NO MORE TWIST.

From then on began the luck of the Tailor of Gloucester. Never
were seen such ruffles and embroidered cuffs. But his button-holes
were the greatest triumph - the stitches were so neat and so small
they looked as if they had been made by little mice!

MICE AND TEACUPS

Here are two little mice on the dresser in the Tailor of Gloucester's kitchen. Colour in the picture with paints, felt-tips or crayons, following the letters and the key below to choose your colours.

KEY: **B** = blue   **R** = red   **W** = white   **LB** = light brown
      DB = dark brown   **Y** = yellow   **G** = green

6 TAILOR OF GLOUESTER WORD SQUARE

The Tailor of Gloucester's workshop is full of busy mice, helping him finish the Mayor's wedding coat: There are the names of 24 items which can all be found in his shop. Can you find and circle all the words? One word has been found already, and to help you all the words are listed below.

R	P	T	T	A	B	L	E	A	B	U	T	T	O	N
A	I	X	R	H	Q	A	R	L	B	V	A	S	M	O
S	N	O	I	P	R	C	Y	C	F	D	E	P	I	T
T	C	I	M	O	F	E	L	T	P	S	W	A	W	T
A	U	V	M	P	A	E	A	M	W	I	C	R	U	O
P	S	S	I	L	K	R	M	D	O	B	N	C	B	C
E	H	I	N	O	N	C	T	Q	I	L	D	S	R	M
M	I	Y	G	V	O	N	P	M	R	U	F	F	L	E
E	O	P	S	A	T	I	N	D	O	B	X	R	P	O
A	N	W	R	E	S	B	E	L	N	U	L	A	M	P
S	R	T	A	H	F	P	E	R	M	P	E	S	I	Q
U	M	B	C	R	I	O	D	T	I	O	R	E	R	E
R	I	N	Q	T	E	V	L	E	V	X	G	P	R	D
E	E	L	E	A	T	H	E	R	M	P	F	O	O	S
B	O	W	T	R	Y	Q	S	C	I	S	S	O	R	S

TAPE MEASURE	MIRROR	BUTTON	FELT
PIN CUSHION	LAMP	PINS	SILK
BENCH	IRON	TABLE	KNOTS
LEATHER	RUFFLE	TRIMMINGS	LACE
VELVET	SCRAPS	SATIN	BOW
SCISSORS	COTTON	NEEDLES	THREAD

54

MOUSE TAILOR

Look at this mouse, sitting on a cotton reel on the Tailor of Gloucester's workbench. Paint or colour the picture, following the letter and the key below to choose your colours.

KEY: **B** = blue   **R** = red   **W** = white   **LB** = light brown
        DB = dark brown   **Y** = yellow   **G** = green

7 UNINVITED GUESTS

Poor Mrs Tittlemouse! Will she ever get her home clean and tidy? All sorts of visitors keep interrupting her cleaning. Fill in this crossword to see who they are; the pictures will give you some clues too. (If you'd like to read about Mrs Tittlemouse and other Beatrix Potter characters, there is a list of Tales at the back of this book.)

CLUES

Down

1 Beautiful wings for fluttering by
2 A friend of Miss Muffet's
3 A hard black shell and dirty feet

Across

1 'Zizz bizz ' say a swarm of these
2 He lives in a pond like a frog
3 A little old woman in a red spotty cloak

SIMPKIN IN THE SNOW

Paint or colour this picture of Simpkin, who has wandered out into the snow while the Tailor of Gloucester is sleeping.

Poor Simpkin felt very lonely when he was wandering about in the snow. From the rooftops and the cellars of Gloucester came a thousand merry voices singing the old Christmas rhymes. Every one was celebrating - except poor hungry Simpkin.

Answers

1 A Dinner Party

onions; lard; roast duck; potatoes; mint; parsley; oats; thyme; eggs

Jemima is wearing a bonnet

2 A Fishing Expedition

Mr Alderman Ptolemy Tortoise has the fish; Sir Isaac Newton has the shoe; Mr Jeremy Fisher has the basket

3 A Picture Letter

letter; money; shop; cheese; bacon; months; box; candles; Tiggy-winkle; chocolate; box; pocket; money; policeman

4 Washing Day

e Benjamin Bunny

c Pigling Bland

a Tom Kitten

b Timmy Tiptoes

d Jemima Puddle-duck

f Samuel Whiskers

5 Peter Rabbit

1 There are only two flower-pots

2 Three of the apples are missing

3 Only one onion is left by the watering-can

4 Mr McGregor has lost his hat

5 The buttons have come off Peter Rabbit's jacket

6 One of the birds has flown away

6 Word Square

```
R P T T A B L E A B U T T O N
A I X R H Q A R L B V A S M O
S N O I P R C Y C F D E P I T
T C I M O F E L T P S W A W T
A U V M P A E A M W I C R U O
P S S I L K R M D O B N C B C
E H I N O N C T Q I L D S R M
M I Y G V O N P M R U F F L E
E O P S A T I N D O B X R P Q
A N W R E S B E L N U L A M P
S R T A H F P E R M P E S I Q
U M B C R I O D T I O R E R E
R I N Q T E V L E V X G P R D
F E L E A T H E R M P F O O S
B O W T R Y Q S C I S S O R S
```

7 Uninvited Guests

Down	Across
1 butterfly	1 bees
2 spider	2 toad
3 beetle	3 ladybird

Here is a complete list of some other Beatrix Potter books you may enjoy:

THE ORIGINAL PETER RABBIT BOOKS